MR. TICKLE
and the Scary Halloween

Roger Hargreaves

Original conce
Roger Hargre

Written and illustrated by
Adam Hargreaves

EGMONT

There was a time, Mr Tickle thought to himself, when Halloween was fun.

But not any more.

Not since Little Miss Scary had moved to town.

Now, Halloween was downright scary.

Scare your pants off scary.

Last year, Little Miss Scary had scared the smile off Mr Happy.

She had scared the bows off Little Miss Giggles.

And she had even scared the hat off Mr Brave!

Little Miss Scary had scared everyone.

"But this year will be different!" said Mr Tickle to himself.

Little Miss Scary was very excited about Halloween this year.

She had everything ready. As she left her house to go trick or treating, she couldn't help chuckling to herself.

Oh, what fun she was going to have!

Her first victim was Little Miss Dotty.

And the plan for Little Miss Dotty was to creep up behind her and drop a huge plastic spider on her head.

But as she sneaked up behind Little Miss Dotty there was something sneaking up behind her.

An extraordinarily long thing.

A thing that tickled her.

Little Miss Scary burst out laughing.

And as you most probably know, it is very difficult to be scary when you are laughing.

"Hello, Little Miss Scary," said Little Miss Dotty. "I like your spider. Are you going to a Halloween party?"

Little Miss Scary was cross that her scary trick hadn't worked. She stomped off without saying a word.

Little Miss Scary's next trick was to paint herself with glowing paint and swing on a rope from the branch of a tree.

But as she sat on the branch waiting for Mr Bump to come by, that extraordinarily long something reached up into the tree and tickled her again.

She laughed so much that she fell right out of the tree!

Shortly afterwards Mr Bump found her swinging upside down.

"Hello, Little Miss Scary," laughed Mr Bump. "That looks like the sort of thing that happens to me!"

Little Miss Scary could only scowl.

Every time Little Miss Scary tried to scare someone, something would tickle her.

Now, we all know who that was, don't we? But Little Miss Scary could not work it out.

It was turning out to be a very frustrating Halloween.

And so it went on all night.

She had planned to cover Little Miss Neat in green goo, but she laughed so much she spilt it over herself.

She was going to scare Mr Quiet by creeping up behind him and banging two dustbin lids together, but she laughed so much she fell in one of the bins and got stuck.

And she was going to scare Mr Grumpy with a rubber bat, but she was laughing so much even Mr Grumpy thought it was funny!

On her way home, Little Miss Scary met Mr Tickle.

"How was your Halloween?" asked Mr Tickle.

"Not much fun," replied Little Miss Scary, gloomily.
"Not so much trick or treating as …"

"… tickle treating?" suggested Mr Tickle.

And he laughed so much that tears rolled down his face.